How to Use the Projector

- Pick a clear space on a light-coloured wall or ceiling one to one-and-a-half metres away.

- The biggest image can be seen when the projector is one-and-a-half metres from the wall or ceiling.

- Use Disk 1 to begin. Change disks as indicated in the story.

- Slide the picture disk into the slot in the top of the projector as shown.

- Turn the disk to the right as you read through the story. The numbers next to the text correspond to the numbers on the projected images. Use the focusing ring to focus the pictures.

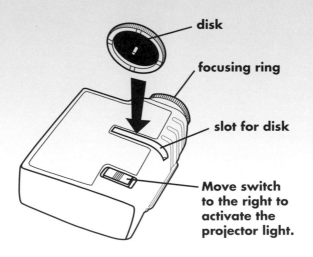

disk

focusing ring

slot for disk

Move switch to the right to activate the projector light.

The Search Is On!

Book 1

adapted by Bill Scollon
illustrated by the Disney Storybook Art Team

White Plains, New York • Montréal, Québec • Bath, United Kingdom

DISK 1

Little Dory lives with her parents in a beautiful coral cave. Dory has a lot of trouble remembering things. Her mum and dad teach her to stay close to home. They worry about Dory getting lost.

One day, her parents' worst fear comes true. Dory swims a little too far from home and is swept far away by the strong undertow!

Lost and alone, Dory stops every fish she sees. Maybe one of them knows her mum and dad. "Hi! I'm Dory. I've lost my family. Can you help me?"

"Where did you see them last?" asks a fish.

Dory thinks. "I can't remember."

Over the years, Dory forgets what she's searching for.

Far out in the ocean, Dory bumps into a clownfish named Marlin. His son, Nemo, is missing. Dory is happy to help Marlin, and together they find Nemo.

Marlin and Nemo invite Dory to live with them on a coral reef. Dory is glad to finally have a home, but her memory loss is still a problem. She often wanders off and forgets where she is going or how to get back. Marlin and Nemo keep a close eye on her.

One day, Dory invites herself on a field trip with Mr. Ray's class. She watches a stingray migration. It's an awesome sight, but Dory gets too close. She is tossed around in their wake and loses consciousness. Dory murmurs, "The Jewel of Morro Bay, California."

When Nemo tells Dory what she said, memories come flooding back. "I remember my family!" she gasps. "We have to find them! Let's go!"

Marlin and Nemo agree to go with her to California. They travel across the ocean through the strong Pacific currents with some sea turtles.

DISK 2

During the journey, a giant squid chases the three friends, and Dory gets tangled up in plastic.

They arrive in Morro Bay and come to the surface to find that they are near the Marine Life Institute—an aquarium devoted to helping sick and injured sea animals. Suddenly, a human pulls Dory out of the water! Marlin and Nemo watch in horror as the human untangles Dory and puts her in a cooler. Marlin knows he has to find and rescue their friend.

Dory is taken to Quarantine and a tag is put on her fin. An octopus named Hank tells Dory she has found the Jewel of Morro Bay.

Dory is almost home! But Hank says the tag on her fin marks her for transfer to Cleveland, an aquarium far away.

"I can't go to the Cleveland," shouts Dory. "I have to find my family."

DISK 3

Hank tries to grab Dory's tag. He wants to go to the Cleveland aquarium, otherwise, he'll be released back into the ocean. "I have extremely unpleasant memories of that place," he tells Dory. She agrees to give Hank her tag if he'll help find her parents. Hank scoops Dory into a nearby coffee jug and carries her to a map of the Institute.

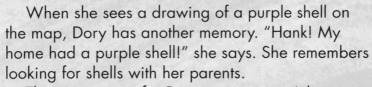

When she sees a drawing of a purple shell on the map, Dory has another memory. "Hank! My home had a purple shell!" she says. She remembers looking for shells with her parents.

There is no time for Dory to continue. A human is coming—they have to hide! Dory spots a bucket with words on the side. "Deeesstinyyy. Destiny!" Dory reads. "We've gotta get in the bucket!"

Without a second thought, Dory flips into the bucket and finds herself surrounded by lots of silver fish that seem to be sleeping.

The bucket of fish is food for a whale shark named Destiny—and she remembers Dory!

"We'd talk through the pipes when we were little," says Destiny. "We're pipe pals!"

Destiny says Dory is from the Open Ocean exhibit. She can get there by swimming through the pipes. "Take two lefts, swim straight and you'll find it," Destiny tells her.

But Dory's afraid of getting lost. Bailey, a beluga whale, could guide her, but he says his echolocation isn't working.

"And I won't fit," adds Hank. "You have to go by yourself. There's no other way."

Dory has a memory flashback! "My father said, 'There's always another way.' Follow me!"

Hank puts Dory into a cup and climbs into an empty pushchair. The octopus turns the wheels while Dory tells him which way to go. They lose control of the pushchair and it crashes into a ledge. Dory and Hank fly through the air and land in the touch pool.

Little hands grab at Dory and Hank from every direction. "What's the plan?" Dory asks Hank.

"It's too dangerous to move," Hank answers from underneath a rock.

Dory remembers something her dad told her, "Just keep swimming." Dory leads the way as they cross the pool. They weave past screaming sea cucumbers and starfish. Then, it happens—a kid surprises Hank with a hard poke. Hank is horrified to see that he's inked in the water. "That's okay. Everyone does it," Dory says to comfort her friend.

Dory peeks above the surface. The Open Ocean exhibit is straight ahead!

Meanwhile, Marlin and Nemo have been trying to find a way into the Institute. Two sea lions, Fluke and Rudder, offer to help. They have a loon friend named Becky who will fly them there in a bucket! They call her over in Becky talk, "Oo-roo!"

"This is nuts," shouts Marlin as Becky takes off.

As they fly over the Institute, Becky spots spilled popcorn on the ground. She hangs the bucket in a tree and swoops down to eat. "Becky! What are you doing?!" Marlin shouts, afraid that she's forgotten them. "Oo-roo, loo-loo!" he calls frantically.

DISK 4

Marlin scoots the bucket down the branch to get Becky's attention.

"I don't think we should move the bucket," Nemo says. Marlin doesn't listen and the branch snaps back! Marlin and Nemo fly through the air and splash into a tank of toy fish in the gift shop.

Marlin isn't sure what to do next. "What would Dory do?" asks Nemo.

They look around and see a fountain of geysers shooting into the air. They decide to take a chance—just like Dory would. They take a deep breath, leap out of the tank, and skip across the waterspouts in the display outside. Finally, they land in the tidal pool exhibit.

Back in the Institute, Hank carries Dory to the top of the Open Ocean tank. "Well, this is it, kid," he says.

Dory gives Hank her tag. "You know, I think I'm going to remember you," she says.

Hank chuckles. "Ah, you'll forget me in a heartbeat. I'll have a hard time forgetting you, though." Hank gently lowers Dory into the tank. "Now, go get your family." Hank gently drops her in the tank, sad to see her go.

Continued in Book 2...

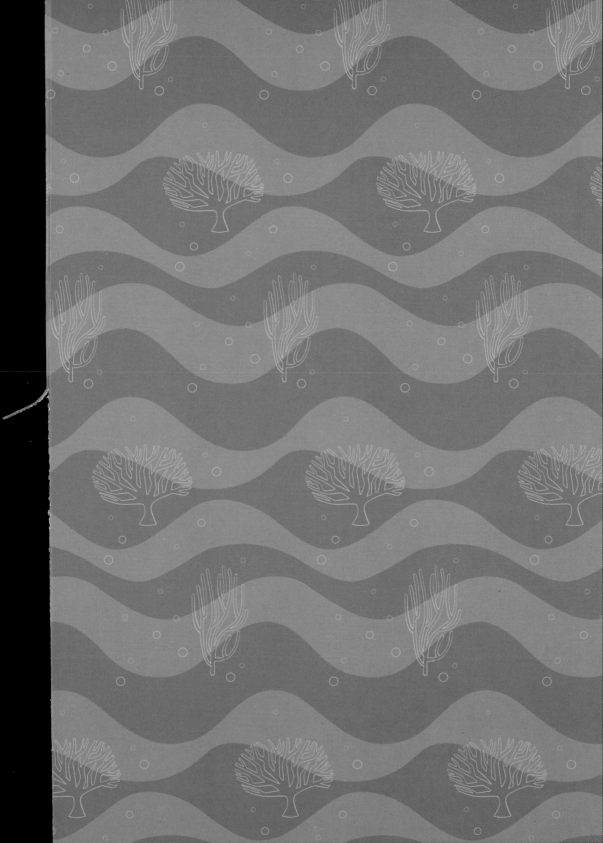